Copyright © 1991 by Françoise and Frédéric Joos.
This special paperback edition first published in 2003 by Andersen Press Ltd.
The rights of Françoise and Frédéric Joos. to be identified as the author and illustrator of this work
have been asserted by them in accordance with the Copyright, Designs and Patents Act, 1988.
First published in Great Britain in 1991 by Andersen Press Ltd. 20 Vauxhall Bridge Road, London SW1V 2SA.
Published in Australia by Random House Australia Pty., 20 Alfred Street, Milsons Point, Sydney, NSW 2061.
All rights reserved. Colour separated in Switzerland by Photolitho AG, Zürich.
Printed and bound in China.

10   9   8   7   6   5   4   3   2   1

British Library Cataloguing in Publication Data available.

ISBN 1 84270 257 2

This book has been printed on acid-free paper

THE GOLDEN SNOWFLAKE

Written by Françoise Joos
Illustrated by Frédéric Joos

Andersen Press · London

Once, a long time ago, there lived a little snowman called
Hector. Like all snowmen at that time, Hector lived in
a vast and very cold country called the Frozen Land.

One evening, before bed, Hector's mother told
him the story of the golden snowflake.

"Every hundred years," she said, "somewhere amongst the millions of white snowflakes that fall there is one little yellow flake that shines like a golden sun.
If a snowman finds a flake like this," she continued, "he is the luckiest snowman alive, because from that moment on nothing can make him melt."

Hector was amazed at the story. He was so excited he couldn't sleep and as he watched the snow fall that night he thought he saw a magnificent golden flake fall far away in the forest.

The next morning Hector was sure he had seen
the golden flake. He asked all his friends to come
and look with him but they couldn't be bothered.
"Silly old Hector," cried Basil. "You'll believe anything."
"Alright then, I'll go on my own," said Hector.

Anyway, it was Wednesday, and Hector usually
went to visit the forest animals on Wednesdays. It
wasn't very far, so Hector set off happily saying
goodbye to his mother.
"Be careful and don't be late back," she said.

Chouchou, the owl, saw him set off and flew ahead to warn the others. Caribou, Fox and all his friends were waiting in the forest clearing when he arrived.

"Did you see anything unusual last night?" asked Hector
straight away. But no, no-one had noticed anything,
so Hector told them the story of the golden snowflake.
"Let's all look," cried Owl,

and together they all hurried to Bear's house to collect
a picnic and tools. Then they ran to the spot where
Hector had seen the golden snowflake fall.

They searched and searched and sifted through heaps
and heaps of snow. As they looked they chatted about
everything that was happening in the forest.

When Bear called 'Lunch is ready,' they were starving,
but they had seen no sign of the golden snowflake. In
his enormous thermos Bear had brought hot chocolate
for everyone . . . except Hector of course. He had
strawberry ice cream instead, which wasn't so bad.

But Hector sighed deeply. "If I had the golden flake, I could drink hot chocolate without melting," he said.

"You could do lots of things," said Fox. "You could come on holiday with us to the beach and have a barbeque."

"I'd teach you everything about bees and honey,"
said Bear.

"I'd take you to listen to the song of the wind in the great birch forests," said Caribou. Everyone had their own plans for Hector.

Just then, Chouchou, who was scientifically-minded, asked, "When you find your flake, how are you going to make it work?"
"I think you should swallow it," said Bear.

"No, no!" said Hector. "You press the flake to your heart until you feel all warm inside and then you will never melt. That is, unless you want to," he added mischievously.

Crow interrupted the conversation. "It's time we were going home. Eat up the rest of the strawberry ice cream, Hector, and we'll walk with you to the edge of the forest."

Even though they hadn't found anything they had
all had great fun that day and planned to meet
the very next Wednesday and look again. And as
Hector, feeling a little disappointed, started for
home, it began to snow.

It was then, just when he
was least expecting it, that
a tiny golden miracle
settled quietly on him.

For according to the
legend that his mother
had told him, if you
dream your dream
hard enough, however
wild it may be, your
wish will come true.

More Andersen Press paperback picture books!

MICHAEL
by Tony Bradman and Tony Ross

THE SANDAL
by Tony Bradman and Philippe Dupasquier

OUR PUPPY'S HOLIDAY
by Ruth Brown

DOTTIE
by Peta Coplans

FRIGHTENED FRED
by Peta Coplans

NO MORE TELEVISION
by Philippe Dupasquier

A COUNTRY FAR AWAY
by Nigel Gray and Philippe Dupasquier

I'LL TAKE YOU TO MRS COLE
by Nigel Gray and Michael Foreman

THE MONSTER AND THE TEDDY BEAR
by David McKee

THERE'S A HOLE IN MY BUCKET
by Ingrid and DieterSchubert

ELEPHANT AND CROCODILE
by Max Velthuijs

THE LONG BLUE BLAZER
by Jeanne Willis and Susan Varley